Written by Gail Herman
Illustrated by the Disney Storybook Art Team

For information address Disney Press, 1101 Flower Street, Glendale, California 91201.

Printed in China
First Box Set Edition, September 2017
3 5 7 9 10 8 6 4 2

ISBN 978-1-368-01490-8
FAC-023680-19025

This book was printed on paper created from a sustainable source

For more Disney Press fun, visit www.disneybooks.com

Nighttime of Fires

Book Five

Disney PRESS

Los Angeles • New York

It was late at night, but Hiro Hamada was wide awake. He was working in his lab at the San Fransokyo Institute of Technology.

Hiro hunched over his computer. He was trying to solve a problem, but nothing was working. Frustrated, he leaned back in his chair. The chair tipped over, throwing Hiro to the ground.

"Ouch!" he cried.

Baymax, Hiro's personal health-care companion, stepped forward. Baymax was a robot built by Hiro's older brother, Tadashi. It was Baymax's job to help people when they were injured.

"I was alerted to your need for help when you said 'ouch,'" Baymax said. "On a scale of one to ten, how would you rate your pain?"

"I'm fine, Baymax," Hiro said quickly, getting up.

Baymax scanned Hiro from top to bottom. "Your energy levels are low. You appear to need rest. Sleep is essential for good health and for mental acuity."

Without another word, Baymax turned and left the lab. When he came back, he was holding a glass of warm milk. "The average fourteen-year-old needs approximately nine point two hours of sleep each night," he said, pointing to a sleep chart that had appeared on the display on his stomach. Baymax held out the glass of milk. "Milk contains enzymes that aid in relaxation and help patients fall asleep."

Hiro rubbed his eyes. "I can't sleep, Baymax! I need to finish this. It's important."

Hiro was building a high-tech firefighting device. It would scan the city for the first signs of fire and shoot a stream of chemicals at the flame to put it out. The chemical mixture would also prevent another fire from starting.

"I don't want anyone else to—" Hiro stopped short, thinking about his brother. Tadashi had died in a fire.

"If you finish the project, will it help you sleep?" Baymax asked.

"Yes," Hiro said. "But I can't seem to get it right. Watch." Hiro sat back down at his computer and pressed some buttons. In a special testing chamber in the corner of his lab, a few pieces of paper in a trash can began to smoke. Hiro typed more instructions. His firefighting device lifted into the air. But by the time it reached the papers, the smoke had turned into a full-blown fire.

"See?" Hiro said to Baymax. "It's way too slow."

The device sprayed a green liquid at the can. The fire sputtered out, but a horrible odor filled the air. The container was melting!

"Plus, the spray is so strong it ruins everything it touches," Hiro said. He entered the testing chamber to examine the damage and accidentally stepped in the melted plastic.

"Ouch! Hot!" Hiro cried, hopping on one foot.

Baymax scanned Hiro again. "Your neural indicators show extreme agitation. You will not be able to sleep in this state."

Hiro picked up his device and examined it closely. What could make it move faster? What would fix the spray?

Just then, the door to Hiro's lab burst open and his friends walked in. Go Go, Wasabi, and Honey Lemon were also students at the San Fransokyo Institute of Technology. They had been hard at work in their labs, too. Their friend Fred had been hanging out with them. Along with Hiro and Baymax, they formed the superhero group Big Hero 6.

"Hey, man," Fred said. "Looks like you could use some help!"

Hiro shook his head. "No one helped Tadashi build Baymax. No offense, guys. I just want to do this alone. Besides, you have your own projects to think about."

Hiro held open the door to his lab and waited for his friends to leave. Then he shut the door behind them and locked it.

"Your stress level has increased," Baymax told Hiro. "Perhaps you would like that glass of milk."

"Not now, Baymax," Hiro said. He had work to do.

Hiro mixed chemicals together and worked up a new model. Then he placed the device back in the testing chamber.

In the chamber, a piece of wood began to glow red-hot. The new device tracked the smoke and sprayed the burning ember. With a hiss, the fire went out.

"Not bad," Hiro said. Suddenly, the wood burst into flames!

Hiro pressed a button. Water poured down, putting the fire out.

Outside the lab, Hiro's friends watched as he tried dozens of different devices and chemical combinations. Finally, Baymax stepped in front of Hiro. "Studies show that brainstorming with friends is useful when solving problems," he said.

Hiro looked at his friends. "You're right, Baymax. Let them in."

Baymax opened the door, and Go Go, Honey, Fred, and Wasabi fell into the room in a jumbled heap.

Fred popped up first. He put his arm around Hiro. "We were Tadashi's friends, too," he said. "We want to help."

Looking at Fred's lopsided grin, Hiro couldn't help smiling back.

"The rest of the guys have some great ideas," Fred continued. "Take a look at some of the stuff they've come up with."

Go Go flung a silvery disk, which whirled quickly around the room.

"Try changing the shape of your device," she suggested. "Something like this could really move through the flames!"

Wasabi nodded in agreement. "And if you fit the disk with laser beams, it can go directly to the source of the fire!"

Honey hugged Hiro. "I think I know the missing chemical, too. Baymax, may I have that glass of milk?" She poured the milk into a test tube. "Enzymes!"

Using his friends' suggestions, Hiro built a new device. He couldn't wait to try it out!

"Ready!" Hiro said, placing the device in the testing chamber.

Hiro tapped his keyboard, and a pile of papers in one corner of the chamber began to smoke. He hit his keyboard again and another fire lit in the opposite corner.

This was the moment of truth. Could Hiro's device handle both fires?

Hiro's device flew through the air. Using its lasers to find the source of the first fire, it sprayed a white liquid over it. Then it raced to put out the other fire.

Within seconds, the embers died and the smoke cleared. The device had done its job perfectly! It was like there had never even been any flames.

"Yes!" Go Go shouted, pumping her fist in the air.

Honey jumped up and down excitedly.

Wasabi and Fred high-fived each other.

Hiro grinned. "Baymax, milk for everyone!" He raised his glass in a toast: "To the best friends a guy could ask for." He turned to Baymax. "Especially you," he whispered.

As the sun began to rise, Hiro yawned. He said good night to his friends, and then, with Baymax at his side, he trudged home.

Exhausted, Hiro fell into bed. "Hey, buddy, might be a good time for you to recharge, too," he told Baymax.